# CORAL ISLAND

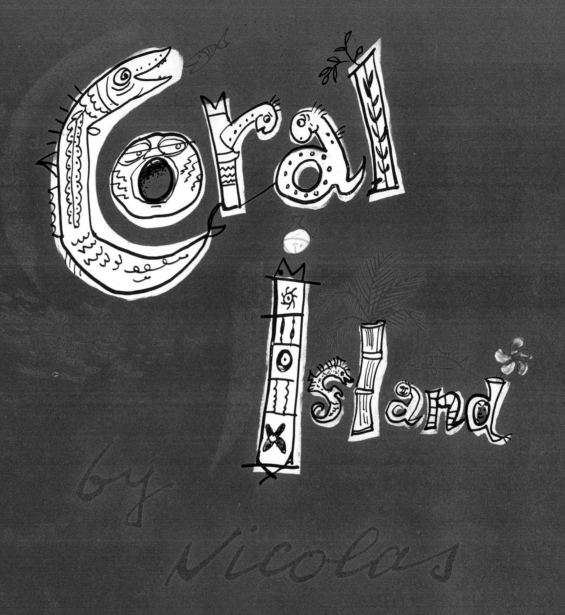

# Coral Island

by

Nicolas

Doubleday & Company, Inc., Garden City, New York

This is the way they say these words
on Coral Island

| Terii | Tare-ee-ee |
|-------|------------|
| Manu | Mah-noo |
| Teopu | Tay-oh-pooh |
| Kaveka | Kah-veh-kah |
| maururu | mah-roo-roo (thank you) |
| mao | mah-oh (a shark) |
| aue | ow-way (an exclamation) |

In the South Seas there is a small island called Coral Island.
From far at sea it looks like a gray-green feathered lizard.
But it is mostly white coral sand, blue-green bushes, and
coconut trees.

A small village of thatched huts is hidden there.

And there is just enough grass to feed one horse.

The horse belongs to Uncle Teopu.

Teopu is the fattest man on the island and by far the best pearl-shell diver.
He is proud of his straw hat, and he is Terii's and Manu's uncle.

Manu plays with the cat, the dog, and the myna bird, and she weaves baskets out of coconut fronds.

Manu's brother, Terii, spends much of his time riding Uncle Teopu's horse.

Kaveka, his pet sea bird, flies above his head at the end of a long fish line.

Terii also spends as much time hanging from a tree branch.

"I am stretching," he explains.
"Why are you stretching?" Manu's eyes widen.
"To grow bigger," Terii says.

Terii wants to grow bigger.

He wants to grow bigger
to become a diver like his uncle Teopu.

One day Uncle Teopu was busy
putting a new fish hook with
a bright red feather on his
straw hat.

"When will I be big enough?"
Terii asked.
"Maybe when this hat will be
worn out," Teopu replied,
patting his round belly.
Then he added with a smile,
"As sharks do not grow smaller,
you will have to grow bigger."

Just then Kaveka and the cat started quarreling about a fish tail.

The bird shrieked, stamped, jumped up and down in a funny way.

And when the cat was least expecting it,
Kaveka snatched the fish tail from under
the cat's paw.

Kaveka flapped his strong white wings and flew up into the air.

The long line that tied Kaveka to a dry twig tightened and tightened.

The twig snapped.

Kaveka flew right over Uncle Teopu's head.

The line caught in the fish hook.
The hat went high in the air with
its red feather sparkling in the sun.

"If the hat flies away is it like being worn out?"
Terii wondered, and he started to run.

"Aue! My hat, my beautiful hat," Teopu screamed,
starting to run the other way after the bird.

Soon the whole village joined Teopu in the chase.

"Uncle Teopu's hat has grown wings." Manu laughed, running heartily on the beach in front of the others.
"Faster! Faster!" Teopu cried, all out of breath. "It's heading for the sea."

They heard the pounding of a gallop on the hard sand.
Uncle Teopu stopped. "That's why Terii ran back." He smiled.

Terii, on horseback, passed them like lightning.
Just in time he caught the hat and pulled Kaveka down to earth.

"Maururu, thank you," Uncle Teopu said.
"Thank you for saving my hat. What can
I do for you, Terii?"
"Can you make me grow bigger?" Terii asked.
"Not quite big enough for a diver," Teopu said,
reshaping his hat, 'but maybe big enough to be
my paddler and to keep an eye on the sharks."

Terii was already racing for the canoe with Kaveka under his arm.

All day long Terii sat in the canoe.
Uncle Teopu blew the air out of his huge chest
with a shrill whistle each time before diving.
Pearl shells piled up around Terii.
Kaveka was swimming nearby like an ordinary duck.

The gentle rocking of the canoe made Terii sleepy.
He dozed, dreaming of a shark eating Uncle Teopu's hat.

Suddenly Kaveka flew up with a shriek that meant danger.

Terii half opened his eyes, blinking in the sun.

What was this dark shape rippling the water, moving silently toward the canoe?

"Mao, a shark," Terii murmured sleepily.

Uncle Teopu was just coming up for a deep breath.
Was all this in the dream?
Terii saw the double row of sharp white teeth ready to close on his uncle's arm.

Terii sprang to his feet. Half awake, he grabbed Teopu's hat
and, diving into the water, he flipped the hat right on the shark's nose.

"Aue," Uncle Teopu sighed with relief when he and Terii were safely back in the canoe. "Aue, it was a good hat, but this shark will wear it out in no time."

"Does that make me bigger?" Terii asked with a gleam in his eyes. Teopu smiled. "If you are big enough to fool a shark, maybe you are big enough to become a diver very soon."

That night on Coral Island there was a feast in Terii's honor.

Kaveka had more fish than he could eat. Even the horse, the dog, the cat,

And Terii danced with Manu.